WITNESS

Todd knelt down. The old man's eyes were opening and closing and blood was running from his nose. He looked dazed, as if he had no idea where he was.

'It's all right, Mr Wilson,' Todd said, pulling some tissues out of his pocket and pressing them into the old man's hand. 'It's me, Todd Lucas. I used to do a paper round for you.'

Jason Ripley was far away, half-walking, half-running towards a bus that had stopped at the traffic lights. Todd swore under his breath. Then he took his mobile out and pressed 999.

'Ambulance,' he said to the operator. 'Quick as you can. Someone's been attacked.'

Look out for other exciting stories
in the *Shades* series:

SHADES

WITNESS

Anne Cassidy

Evans

Published by Evans Brothers Limited
2A Portman Mansions
Chiltern St
London W1U 6NR

© Evans Brothers Limited 2005

First published in 2005

British Library Cataloguing in Publication Data
Cassidy, Anne, 1952-
    Witnesses. - (Shades)
    1. Crime - Fiction 2. Witnesses - Fiction 3. Young adult
    fiction
    I. Title
    823. 9'14 [J]

    ISBN-10: 0237529246

13-dight ISBN (from January 2007) 978 0 237 52934 6

Series Editor: David Orme
Editor: Julia Moffatt
Designer: Rob Walster

Contents

Chapter One
Late Again

Todd Lucas was twenty minutes late for school when he saw the attack.

It was a wet Monday morning and he was minding his own business. He had his mobile out and was getting ready to send a message to Dex, his best mate. He knew that Dex would be sitting in assembly listening to the Head of Year ramble on.

He smiled to himself. Being late had saved him from that. He looked down at his new trainers. It was the first time he had worn them. He'd had to thread the laces just right. These things took time. He hadn't been able to rush it.

A loud crashing sound made him jump. He spun round and saw the window of *Wilson's Food and Wines* shatter. A man burst out of the door. He was tall and well built, wearing a short leather zip-up jacket. He stopped and looked around and his eyes rested on Todd. For a moment Todd stiffened. The man's face was familiar. Todd was sure he knew him. The man glanced away though, and walked on quickly, shoving both hands in the pockets of his leather jacket. Todd tried to remember the man's name but just then Mr Wilson staggered out of the shop shouting and stumbling.

'Stop! You, stop! I've rung the police. They're coming.'

The man in the leather jacket turned and marched back towards Mr Wilson. He grabbed hold of the old man by his tie.

'I told you to shut up!' he hissed.

Then he pulled one arm back and punched Mr Wilson on the cheek. Todd heard the crack as the older man seemed to fold up and fall on the ground. The man turned and ran away.

Todd hurried towards Mr Wilson. He suddenly remembered who the attacker was. Mr Ripley. He'd been one of the assistant caretakers in his primary school, years before. *Mr Jason Ripley.*

He knelt down. The old man's eyes were opening and closing and blood was running from his nose. He looked dazed, as if he had no idea where he was.

'It's all right, Mr Wilson,' Todd said, pulling some tissues out of his pocket and pressing them into the old man's hand. 'It's me, Todd Lucas. I used to do a paper round for you.'

Jason Ripley was far away, half-walking, half-running towards a bus that had stopped at the traffic lights. Todd swore under his breath. Then he took his mobile out and pressed 999.

'Ambulance,' he said to the operator. 'Quick as you can. Someone's been attacked.'

Chapter Two
Being a Grass

'Just sign there,' PC Roberts said.

Todd paused. He looked at the policeman sitting opposite. He was a thin man with pale white skin and silver-grey hair. On his forehead was a scar shaped like a tick. Todd tried not to look at it. He knew him. The policeman had visited his school a couple of times. Some kids called him

Scarface behind his back.

Todd signed the piece of paper on the bottom line. Then he looked at his watch. Eleven ten. He was well and truly late for school. His form teacher would want an explanation.

'You did well,' PC Roberts said, reading over the typed words. 'We know this Jason Ripley and his family. It won't be long before we pick him up.'

PC Roberts put the statement into a pink folder and then placed the lid back on to his pen. Todd stood up and patted his pockets. He fished out his mobile and looked at the screen. Three missed calls.

'I don't want anyone to know about this,' he said, pointing at the folder with the statement inside.

'Completely confidential,' PC Roberts said.

Todd nodded.

'You should be proud of yourself. You've done Mr Wilson a good turn.'

Policemen and teachers always said stuff like that. Be honest, do the right thing. Todd knew it wasn't always as simple as that.

Todd had been a witness before. When he was on his paper round he'd seen two kids breaking in the side window of a line of cars. He'd seen a couple of men selling drugs on the streets leading to school. He'd seen a fight between two drivers who were involved in an accident.

He'd never gone to the police though. He wasn't a grass. He wasn't exactly a *saint* himself, after all. Life was just easier if you didn't get involved.

Mr Wilson was different. Todd *knew* him. He *liked* him. He had worked for Mr Wilson for about six weeks just before the previous Christmas. The job hadn't lasted long because Todd couldn't stand the early hours. He'd liked the old man. Mr Wilson was a good boss, cheerful and generous. On payday he gave Todd free magazines. He'd given them all a Christmas bonus. His wife, Mrs Wilson, was always singing songs along with the radio. She smoked too much and Mr Wilson said she would die before he did. His son, Terry, had been to every single West Ham football game for twenty odd years. Mr Wilson was a nice old man. He hadn't deserved to be beaten up in the street.

Todd had had no choice but to talk to the police. Dex would be the first to agree. He wasn't sure what Louise would think.

He got on the bus and sat by a window. He looked out at the passing streets and remembered when Jason Ripley had worked in his primary school. The other caretakers were friendly but Mr Ripley was in a constant bad mood, swearing at the school kids when no one else was around. He left suddenly and was replaced by a thin woman in dungarees and big boots. Todd had completely forgotten about him until that day.

The bus stopped and he got off. He hurried towards the back gate. He wanted to get into school unnoticed and then he could say that he'd been there all morning. He'd done it before.

'Todd!'

A voice shrieked along the corridor. He turned round and saw Louise, Lindy and Dex walking in his direction. Louise and Lindy were holding camcorders. Dex had a clipboard and a pen.

'Where you been?' Louise shouted.

'Sssh...' Todd said, 'I'll tell you later.'

He joined them and walked along. He was frowning. He hadn't wanted to be noticed. Now he was walking in between two six-foot tall black girls and a small thin white boy with giant glasses. The whole school would see them.

The next day Todd and Dex were making their way to school. Early for once.

'Louise likes you,' Dex said.

'I know,' Todd said.

'No, I mean, she *lusts* after you.'

Todd sighed. Louise had started hanging round with them a few weeks before. He liked her. She was funny and chatty and knew tons about football. He had a feeling she wanted to be more than just mates. Every now and again she stood a little too close to him. She put her hand on his arm and fixed his collar if it wasn't straight. It made him feel awkward. And she had a strange silent friend called Lindy who listened a lot but said little.

'Todd Lucas!'

Todd stopped and turned to see one of the year twelves walking towards him. It was Michelle something or other. He was puzzled.

'I got a message for you from my cousin,' she said. 'His name's Stephen Ripley. He says you know his brother.'

Stephen Ripley? Todd didn't know anyone of that name. Then he remembered. Ripley. *Jason Ripley*. The man who attacked Mr Wilson. A feeling of gloom settled on him.

'What's the message?' Todd said.

'Stephen said you'll be seeing him. Sooner than you think.'

Chapter Three
Chip-Boy Stephen

After school Todd was waiting for a bus
with Louise and Lindy.

'Why is Dex so small and so thin?'
Louise said.

'He was born small. Three months early.
He only weighed two pounds.'

'Two pounds! Like a bag of sugar! Is that
why he takes so many drugs?'

Todd laughed. Louise made Dex sound like an addict. He had his asthma inhalers and some tablets for stomach problems. Plus his mum bought him tons of vitamins to take.

'Still, no one picks on him. Not when he's a mate of yours,' she said.

Lindy nodded.

Todd thought about it. She was right. Todd wasn't Mr Universe but he could handle himself. He didn't look for fights but he didn't walk away from them either. He'd seen off a couple of older boys who thought they could shove him around. Then there was the Big Fight in Mugger's Alley. That had helped his reputation. He'd ended up losing a front tooth and having a black eye but he'd shrugged it off. People usually left him and Dex alone. Except for Louise and Lindy of course.

Lindy had moved away and Louise was leaning against him. She wasn't really six foot tall but she was big. She had to be. Her school bag weighed a ton. On her shoulder was the camcorder case. She'd taken it home. She was always working on something, a project or an essay. This time it was a film that she, Lindy and Dex were making for Media.

'How is old Wilson? Have you heard?'

'Not good. He's had a small stroke.'

'No!'

'Jason Ripley is on remand. He'll have to go to trial.'

'You'll be a witness?'

'I got no choice,' he said.

Todd would have to go to the courtroom and point at Jason Ripley. The thought of it made him feel anxious. He wasn't *afraid* of Jason Ripley. Not really. He just wanted to do it right. So that Mr Wilson would feel safe in future.

A red Ford pulled up sharply across the road from the bus stop. Its brakes squealed. Todd frowned. A car door swung open. A kid got out and marched up to them.

'You Todd Lucas?' he demanded.

Todd didn't answer. He looked at the kid. He was about the same height as him but a lot heavier. His hair was cropped short and his skin was whiter than white. His left eyelid was heavy as if he had a sty. He was wearing a denim jacket done up to the neck. Some of the buttons had to stretch. Todd recognised him. He worked in the chip shop near the library.

'I'm Stephen Ripley. You grassed my brother up!'

Todd stiffened. He moved his feet so that they were apart. He squared his shoulders.

Stephen Ripley was taking a deep breath. His mouth was small and mean.

'So?' Todd said, edging away from Louise.

'You grassed my brother.'

A car door slammed and Todd looked up to see someone else get out of the Ford. A tall kid who walked towards him. He had something in his hand. Todd sighed. It looked like the leg of a table.

'Oh no,' Louise said.

'Can't get yourself a nice *white* girlfriend?' Stephen Ripley said.

Some of the other kids at the bus-stop laughed. Todd felt his back harden. That was it. It was one thing having a go at him. But not at his mates.

Todd raised both his hands and gave the kid an almighty shove so that he fell back on to the pavement. Then, quick as a flash, Todd squatted down, pushed the boy over and held his arm up his back. The other kid was standing still, holding the table leg up in the air.

'Touch me with that and I'll break his arm,' Todd said.

The other kid looked like he might ignore him so Todd pushed at the arm. Ripley gurgled out some words and the other kid stepped back and lowered the wood.

'Don't threaten me,' Todd said, 'I don't grass on no one but your brother picked on an old man.'

With a last shove Todd stood up and watched as Ripley scrambled to his feet cradling his arm.

'You'll see me again, Lucas!' Ripley shouted, walking back to the car.

'Can't wait. Bring us a portion of chips next time!' Todd said.

The Ford drove off and Todd leaned back

against the bus shelter. Louise moved up beside him. She linked her arm through his.

'You're shaking,' she said.

He shrugged. Then she planted a kiss on his cheek. He felt himself go red and hoped she didn't expect him to do anything in return.

The bus appeared. He gave Louise a weak smile as he stepped on. Inside he wasn't feeling good. Stephen Ripley. He would see him again, he was sure.

Chapter Four
Attacked

Todd's mobile was ringing. He hoped it
wasn't Louise. Since that day at the bus
stop she'd been popping up everywhere.
Four days of Louise and Lindy at his elbow.
Three or four text messages every night.
It was driving him mad.

He pressed the button and saw that it
was Dex's home phone.

'I'm not going to school today. We need to talk. Something's happened. Can you come round?'

'Sure.'

It was twenty past nine. Todd was running a bit late. He just had time to pop into Dex's house and still get in for period two. His form tutor would never know. He sat on his bed and slipped his feet into his trainers and began to lace them up, taking care that each lace was the exact same length.

He thought about Dex.

A lot of people wondered why he and Dex were mates. That was easy. Dex moved in five doors away from Todd and they'd gone to secondary school together. They'd been in different form classes but always met up to walk home and discuss the day. They weren't *mates* but they knew each other well.

They were the same size then. Todd shot up though and Dex seemed to stay small. In year ten they saw less of each other. They were doing different options and Todd got in with a couple of rough boys while Dex hung about with the computer crowd. They nodded to each other but Todd found his new friends more exciting.

His mates were two kids who were both called Jack. They spent a lot of time drifting round the shopping mall. When they left they usually had a load of stuff that hadn't been paid for. CDs. DVDs. Sweets. Pens. Magazines. Anything that could be hidden up sleeves or down trousers or in the lining of a jacket. At first Todd thought it was fun, *dangerous*. But then he started to feel bad about it. One of the Jacks started talking about more serious crimes. He didn't like it and drifted away from them. That's when he had the paper round. A legal way of making money. He even tried a few other mates but didn't quite fit in anywhere.

The two Jacks saw him around, invited him out, kept phoning him up. In the end he agreed to go out one evening. The two Jacks promised him a bit of fun and Todd knew that it would mean breaking the law in some way. Even though he had a heavy heart he agreed to go. Why not? It never seemed to worry them.

He went out about seven and headed for the town centre. He took a short cut through an alley that ran down the back of the shops. It wasn't a good place to be. Many of the lights were frequently broken and there were big wheelie bins along the way which belonged to the shops. They were perfect hiding places for people intent on stealing or violence. It was nicknamed Mugger's Alley and sensible kids avoided it.

But Todd was running late. He didn't want to go the safe way, past the shops, past the library, through the bus station. It meant a much longer walk. So he put his hands in his pockets, squared his shoulders and walked through Mugger's Alley.

It was dark and some of the giant bins had been moved so that they blocked the path. He edged around them and up ahead saw a small knot of kids near the far end. They were moving in and out of a space behind some of the bins. There were some nasty sounds and he thought it might be a fight. He put his head down, determined to ignore what was happening. He was in a hurry. He had somewhere he had to be.

There were three boys bearing down on someone in the corner behind one of the giant bins. Todd sighed. He couldn't just walk past. Could he? The boys noticed him and swore at him, telling him to get lost. Todd didn't like that for a start. He recognised them. They were from his school. He wasn't going to let them tell him what to do. He stepped sideways and saw Dex sitting on the ground, his back against the wall, his arms held up in front of his face. His books were strewn all over the place and his glasses were smashed.

Todd felt a moment's fury. He grabbed the hood of one of the boys and threw him aside. The boy hit a dustbin and it creaked as it rolled a few inches away. Todd hooked his arm round the neck of the second, squeezing him until the boy cried out for him to stop. The third boy took a punch at Todd's face and caught him a blow on the lip and then another to his cheek. Todd bent over and ran at him, forcing him up against a brick wall. He grabbed the boy's jacket and felt it tear. The boy shouted and when Todd backed off he turned and ran away. The other two followed a second later, their angry voices criss-crossing in the night air.

He helped Dex up. The smaller lad was crying and Todd felt pity for him. He picked up all his computer magazines and his discs and his broken glasses.

'What are you doing here?' Todd said. 'No one comes here. Especially not at night!'

'Computer club. At the library. I was late so I thought I'd go this way.'

'Come on, I'll help you home,' Todd said.

'There's no need,' Dex said, his face red.

'Come on. I didn't have anything special planned.'

Luckily, Dex's mum and dad were out so

he went inside and helped clean Dex up. They messed around on the computer for a while, opening up web sites and setting up a web cam that Dex had just bought. He felt relaxed. He had a good time. When he got to school the next day he found out that the two Jacks had tried to steal another kid's mobile and one of them had been stabbed for his trouble.

There was a big buzz about the Fight. Most kids thought that Todd had saved Dex. But really it was the other way round. Helping Dex had saved him from a possible stabbing and arrest. In a funny kind of way it changed his life.

Dex had a huge brain. He knew everything there was to know about computers. Mostly it was just the two of them. Until Louise and Lindy started hanging round.

Dex opened his front door as soon as Todd rang his bell. Todd was shocked at the sight of his friend. He had a black eye and his shirt was ripped.

'What happened?' he said.

Todd didn't need an answer. He knew straight away what had happened.

Stephen Ripley.

Chapter Five
Blackmail

'What happened?' Todd said again.

They were in Dex's room. Dex put
his finger on his lips. He closed his room
door, then went over and sat down at
his computer.

'I told my mum I fell over,' he explained.

He began moving the mouse around.
He was upset, Todd could tell. He had a

rolled-up flannel that he held up to his injured eye.

'I went out early to get milk.'

Todd listened. He fiddled with his trainer laces while he waited for Dex's story.

'There was no-one about. I was walking past the park entrance and two kids jumped out in front of me.'

Dex picked up a small blue inhaler and puffed into his mouth. Todd felt a heavy feeling in his chest as if someone had stuffed a cushion down there. Dex exhaled.

'I only really looked at the one in front. A big heavy kid with a funny eye.'

Stephen Ripley. Todd knew it.

'He punched me in the face and took my mobile.'

Todd pushed his knuckles against each other, wishing that Ripley's nose was in between.

'He said, "*Tell Todd Lucas I'll be giving him a call.*"'

Todd swore. He walked up and down Dex's room. He should have known that Ripley wouldn't leave it. *He should have known!*

'I'll get you another mobile...'

But Dex was shaking his head, his blue inhaler inside his mouth.

'It doesn't matter,' he said, breathing in and out. 'It's insured.'

Just then Todd's ring tone sounded. He put his hand in his pocket and pulled his mobile out. On the screen was the word *Dex*. He sighed. Ripley was using Dex's mobile to call him.

'What?' he said, abruptly, answering the call.

'That's not a nice way to speak to someone!'

It was Ripley.

'What do you want?' Todd said, his voice flat.

'I had a nice chat with your friend this morning.'

'And?'

Todd didn't trust himself to say more.

'I don't want my brother to go to prison. So what you need to do,' Ripley said, 'is to withdraw your statement from the police. Then I'll give your dwarf mate his mobile back.'

Why did Ripley have to be so nasty? That's what Todd couldn't understand.

'You can chuck the mobile,' he said. 'There's plenty more where that came from.'

'Thing is,' Ripley said, 'it's not just about that. I gave your mate a thump today. Next time I'll break his legs.'

'Then you'll have me to deal with,' Todd said with a fake laugh. 'I didn't see you doing all that well at the bus-stop the other day.'

'Listen Lucas, you can't babysit your mate all the time. When I come to break his legs it'll be at the time that he least expects it. One night, weeks from now, when you and the dwarf think it's all over, I'll be there, waiting round some dark corner.'

Todd cut the call. He felt like throwing his mobile at something. Dex was looking at him.

'What did he say?'

'He wants me to withdraw my statement to the police.'

'You can't do that!' Dex said.

Todd knocked his knuckles together and pictured Ripley behind the counter at the chip shop. He usually just plonked the chips down and grunted. He wasn't happy in his work. Todd imagined himself leaning across the counter, grabbing his white overall and punching his fat cheek.

But that wouldn't help. He knew that Ripley was right. Todd couldn't be with Dex all the time. There would always be a night and a dark corner and poor Dex would have to pay for something Todd had done.

'Are you going to school?' Dex said.

Todd shook his head.

'I'm going to the police station.'

'Just because he did this? You can't!' Dex said, holding the flannel against his bad eye. 'We could report it to the police!'

'Except that it would be his word against yours. And anyway, I tried going to the police about his brother. Look where that got me! No, it's getting out of hand. I've decided. I'm going to withdraw my statement.'

Chapter Six
A Change of Heart

Todd walked briskly past the school gates in the direction of the police station. He hoped there were no teachers looking out of the classroom windows. If he was quick he might still get into school for period three. Then he could say he'd been there all along. His form tutor probably wouldn't notice.

Turning the corner he heard a voice.

'Todd!'

He groaned. It was Louise. That girl had radar for him. Whenever he was around she seemed to appear. He heard her footsteps and then she was at his side. She was on her own for once. She had her hair in thin plaits, pulled up at the back of her head. It looked good. She was holding a camcorder.

'Where you off to?' she said.

'What you doing with that?' he said, ignoring her question.

'Making footage of the streets. It's for our film. It's an advert for the area. Like a holiday brochure, only in film. I'm supposed to be with my group but I slipped off.'

Todd didn't answer. He had things on his mind. He also thought that if he didn't speak she might go back to school. She didn't. She kept walking with him, the camcorder hanging over her shoulder. When they got close to the police station she put her hand on his arm.

'What you doing?' she said.

'I'm changing my statement. Ripley hit Dex and took his mobile. He's threatened to do it again only worse.'

'But you can't. Jason Ripley will get off.'

'No. Maybe not. Mr Wilson saw him as well. When he's better he can identify him. See, it'll be all right. And this way Dex doesn't get bothered.'

He walked into the station. Louise was still behind him. He stopped.

'Louise, I can do this on my own.'

'I'll wait out here. I'll take some film of the police station.'

'I might be a long time.'

'Doesn't matter. I'll wait,' she said.

He went in and stood at the counter.

'Is PC Roberts in?' he said.

Just then a door burst open and PC Roberts walked out into the public area. The policeman looked unhappy. He was doing his jacket up, patting his pockets as if he was looking for something. Todd called his name.

'What's up?' he said, looking at his watch.

'I've come to—'

'I haven't got much time,' he said, pushing his hair back, his fingers brushing across his scar. 'I've just had a phone call from the hospital. George Wilson has died. He had a second stroke this morning. All because of that low life, Ripley.'

'Dead?' Todd said, shocked.

'I'm just about to go and speak to his family. Jason Ripley could get charged with manslaughter for this.'

The policeman went out of the station

doors and Todd followed him. In front of him was Louise holding her camcorder up.

'What can I do for you?'

'It's not important now,' said Todd.

He watched as the policeman walked off to a waiting car. Todd felt a horrible weight on his chest. The old man hadn't recovered. He'd been hit by Jason Ripley and then had two strokes. Now he was dead. How could Todd change his story?

He and Louise were walking slowly back to school. He told her everything.

'Can't you just beat up Stephen Ripley?'

Todd shrugged.

'I could fight him. I could hurt him. But he could still get Dex. Weeks from now he could get his own back. He said he'd break Dex's legs. He might well do that.'

'Tell the police. Scarface. He'll know what to do!'

'I got no evidence. It's Dex's word against Ripley!'

'When's his brother go to court?'

'A couple of weeks, I think. But now that Mr Wilson has died they might charge him again. He could be in court any day. Maybe even tomorrow.'

'Mm...'

Louise was quiet for once. Todd's mind was racing. What could he do? He couldn't withdraw his statement now that poor Mr Wilson was dead. He thought of Mrs Wilson lighting up one cigarette after another and Terry Wilson, showing off his new West Ham replica shirt. How could he let them down? On the other hand there was Dex, his best mate, to think of. How could he get Stephen Ripley to leave Dex alone?

'Which chip shop does Ripley work in?' Louise said.

'The Mermaid,' Todd said.

'Opposite the library? One of the shops that are in front of Mugger's Alley?'

Todd nodded. He wasn't sure why she was asking.

'I've got an idea,' she said. 'Maybe we can trap the chip-shop boy. Trouble is it'll mean Dex being a hero. Do you think he's up to it?'

Todd couldn't answer. *Hero* wasn't a word he would use to describe his best mate.

Chapter Seven
Mugger's Alley

After school Todd walked in the direction of
Dex's house. He was on his own. Louise had said
that it was best that way. He thought about
what he was going to say. Trouble was he knew
that Dex would agree to anything he asked.
He'd do it just to please him. Dex was like that.

But could Todd ask him to put himself
in such danger?

He remembered the night that he had seen Dex beaten up, sprawled out in Mugger's Alley. He'd taken him home, holding his ripped bags with the dirty and torn books inside. Dex had limped a bit and Todd had insisted that he lean on him. He'd gone into Dex's and helped to repair some of his stuff. Not the glasses. They were beyond repair.

He remembered the first few times that they went out together. Dex was nervous, looking round, jumping at the slightest sound. He carried a baseball bat in his bag. Todd knew he'd never use it, but if it made him feel better what was the harm? Dex carried it for months and then one day Todd noticed it standing in the corner of his bedroom. Dex had started to relax.

Now Todd was going to ask him to do something that might change all that.

'I'll do it. 'Course I'll do it,' said Dex. 'You should have told me what Ripley said about breaking my legs. I'm not a baby.'

'I know. I just thought...'

'Just because I got beat up you shouldn't think that I'm a coward. I'm not.'

'I know you're not. I never said you were.'

Dex had sticky tape round the arm of his glasses. His eye and his cheekbone looked red. His mouth was tightly shut though and there was a hardness about him.

'I can't believe Mr Wilson's dead.'

Todd nodded. Dex took a puff of his blue inhaler. After a moment he exhaled.

'A second stroke.'

'After Jason Ripley hit him.'

Dex was quiet for a moment.

'When are we going to do it?'

'Louise is going check that Ripley's working in the shop tonight. She'll text me and then we'll go about seven. When it's dark.'

'No problem!' Dex said, cheerfully.

Later Todd saw Dex put the baseball bat in his bag. It gave him a bad feeling but he didn't say anything.

At six he got a text from Louise.

Chip Boy In Place.

The Mermaid fish shop was lit up brightly. Todd could smell the chips and the vinegar from far away. He gave Louise a call. She and Lindy were already there. They had everything ready.

'I'll ring you as soon as something happens.'

'Is Dex up for it?' she said.

'I think so,' Todd said. He pictured the baseball bat in Dex's bag. It made him feel nervous.

'OK. I'll wait to hear from you.'

Todd followed Dex as he walked along the shopping precinct. He kept his distance and stood behind a van that was parked outside the shop. He had a partial view of the inside of the chip shop. Dex seemed to pause for a moment before going in. Then he walked in and stood by the counter. Todd could see the backs of a couple of customers. After a few moments he saw them leave, dipping their hands into white cones of chips. He felt hungry. Then he felt guilty for even thinking about food.

Would Dex have the courage to confront Stephen Ripley? To challenge him? To entice him outside the shop?

Todd suddenly felt weak and light-headed.

It was a stupid plan. Four fifteen-year-old kids playing at being grown up. It might not work and even if it did there was no guarantee that they would get any evidence. And if they were lucky? Would it be enough evidence for the police to charge Ripley?

He thought of PC Roberts and the scar on his forehead. It made him look like a hard man. He would probably laugh at them all.

At that moment Dex appeared at the door of the shop. Without so much as a look at Todd he turned right and ran along the pavement towards the end of the row of shops. A second later Stephen Ripley flew out of the shop door after him. He was still wearing his overall. He was shouting something. He looked big and white running down the street but his weight meant that he was slower than Dex.

Todd felt panicky. There was no time to call it off. They had to go through with it. He made a quick call to Louise and then ran in the opposite direction. At the end of the shops he turned down towards Mugger's Alley and slowed down.

He walked quietly, his heart thumping. Further up he saw the white overall of Stephen Ripley. He hoped that Louise and Lindy were well hidden. He knew that they would be crouching behind the giant bins. He hoped that Dex had stopped running at the right place.

There was so much that could go wrong!

He crept along the alley with his back to the wall, darting in and out of the dustbins. He could hear Ripley shouting and swearing at Dex. Todd got as close as he could, edging round a dustbin so that he could see what was happening. He held his breath and watched. All the while, he was ready to move, to run and slap Ripley around if it was necessary. He hoped it wasn't necessary.

'You won't break my legs,' Dex said,

loudly, his voice cracking. 'I'll break your legs. With this!'

Dex held the baseball bat high as if he was waiting for someone to throw a ball at him. Ripley let out a laugh and lunged towards him. He grabbed the bat by its other end and pulled it off Dex.

'You can threaten Todd all you like but he's not going to withdraw his statement,' Dex cried. 'Your brother's going to prison. There's nothing you can do about it.'

'I'll tell you what, dwarf. I'll just break one of your legs tonight. Then if your mate doesn't change his statement, I'll come back and break the other one tomorrow!'

Todd felt himself move forward, as if he was on the starting block of a race. He looked hard into the darkness beyond Ripley. He could just see the very top of Louise's hair above the wheelie bin. Lindy was probably behind the next bin. This had to work. It had to work.

Dex didn't stop.

'You're a coward. You won't do it. You couldn't break an egg!'

Stephen Ripley swore and lifted the baseball bat. He swung it behind his head. Dex cried out in agony, as if he'd already been hit. The bat swung down just as Todd let out a loud whistle. The noise distracted the chip-shop boy and the bat hit the wall. He turned around and was faced with Todd and the two girls, each holding a camcorder.

'Smile, Ripley,' Todd said. 'You're a movie star.'

Chapter Eight
Movie Star

The next lunchtime Todd and the others took the film to the police station. PC Roberts took them into a back office and they watched it. Todd had been looking forward to it but he was disappointed when he saw what was on the screen

'I had to use night vision lenses,' Louise explained.

The picture was dark and had a green tint. It was possible to see the shapes of the wheelie bins and shadows. That was it. Mugger's Alley looked like a strange planet.

PC Roberts watched carefully. He asked a number of questions. When Dex came on to the screen, panting past the girls, Todd began to feel a little better. Then came Ripley soon after. What happened next was over very quickly. The screen was filled with Ripley's face. He was holding something in the air but it was hard to see what it was.

Todd groaned to himself. He put his head in his hands. Had it all been for nothing?

'Well, well!' PC Roberts said, pressing the STILL button.

Todd looked up. The frozen image showed Stephen Ripley with a baseball bat above his head. His eyes were glowing. He looked like an alien. His face was recognisable. Just.

PC Roberts pushed the PLAY button and the film played on. His thumb pressed the volume and Stephen Ripley's voice became loud. Louise had set up a remote microphone in one of the bins. It picked up everything that was being said.

'I'll just break one of your legs tonight. Then if your mate doesn't change his statement, I'll come back and break the other one tomorrow.'

'That's interfering with witnesses,' Todd said, excitedly.

'Um...'

PC Roberts didn't answer. The film played on until the end when Ripley turned round to face the camera. Then he ran off.

'You can arrest him for that? Can't you?' Louise said, looking pleased with herself.

But PC Roberts sat looking thoughtful. His hand strayed up to his forehead and he felt along the line of his scar.

'Strictly speaking he's not interfering with witnesses because Dexter, here, was not a witness to anything.'

Dex looked uncomfortable. Todd felt angry, suddenly.

'He beats up Dex and gets away with it!' he said.

'No. It's Threatening Behaviour. Stephen Ripley has done this before a number of times. In the past he's been let off with community service. I was in court with him a month or so ago and the magistrate said it was his last chance. He'll get a custodial sentence this time. No doubt.'

They were all quiet for a moment. PC Roberts pressed the rewind button. They watched as the film started moving backwards at speed. The dark green colours of the alley. Ripley's white overall running backwards past the dark shapes of the wheelie bin. It was another world. Weird.

Todd left the station feeling better than he had for days. Dex was walking ahead with Lindy. There was something different about his friend. He looked taller, or his back was straighter. He was certainly walking fast, his hands swinging at his sides.

The baseball bat had been a nice touch. Todd had thought that Dex took it with him to protect himself. But he had always intended for Ripley to take it off him. *I knew it would make the film more dramatic,* he'd said.

Louise had taken the camcorders into school that morning and edited the film. She had cut it at various points to make it clearer. It had been shaky and dark. But it had done the trick.

'You did a great job,' Todd said to Louise when the others were far ahead.

'OK. I deserve a kiss then!' she said.

Todd felt himself go red but he stopped walking and leant forward to give her a kiss on the lips. Louise looked as though she'd just won a prize.

'We'd better catch up with the others,' he said.

Later the four of them stopped outside *Wilson's Food and Wines*. The shutters were down and there was a notice pinned on the door.

We are closed due to the sad loss of George Wilson. Many thanks for the flowers and sympathy.

Louise was holding a bunch of carnations that they'd bought at the supermarket. She placed it on the pavement in front of the shop. They all stood quietly for a minute.

Then they walked back towards school. Todd looked at his watch. With a bit of luck he wouldn't be late. For once.

Look out for this exciting story
in the *Shades* series:

SHOUTING AT THE STARS

David Belbin

When the show was over, she signed some autographs. A young man, about her age, held out a copy of *New Lad*.

'I don't want to sign that,' she said.

'Why not? You look great in it.' He opened the magazine at her picture. 'Please?'

Layla gave in. 'What do you want me to write?' she asked.

'How about, *For Gary, with love?*'

Layla covered her chest with words.

'Magic! I'm going to put it on the wall above my bed in my hall of residence.'

She looked at Gary. He had long hair and a thin face with a few spots. He wasn't bad looking. A year ago, if he'd asked her out, she would have said "yes".

'Are you at university here?' she asked.

'No. Derby. I came by train. I'm going to see you in Birmingham too. I thought you were great at that festival in Leicester.'

'Thanks a lot,' she said, before speaking to the next in line. The lad was following her around. He had been at the festival. Was he the heckler? If he was, why would he be so nice to her? And why hadn't he called out tonight?